Moon Bubble

George Ivanc
Sue Dani

NELSON
CENGAGE Learning™

Australia • Brazil • Japan • Korea • Mexico • Singapore • Spain • United Kingdom • United States

NELSON
CENGAGE Learning

Moon Bubble

Fast Forward
Emerald Level 25

Text: George Ivanoff
Illustrations: Sue Dani
Editor: Johanna Rohan
Design: Ami Sharpe
Series design: James Lowe
Production controller: Seona Galbally
Audio recordings: Juliet Hill, Picture Start
Spoken by: Matthew King and Abbe Holmes
Reprint: Jennifer Foo

ISBN 978 0 17 012720 2
ISBN 978 0 17 012717 2 (set)

Cengage Learning Australia
Level 7, 80 Dorcas Street
South Melbourne, Victoria Australia 3205
Phone: 1300 790 853

Cengage Learning New Zealand
Unit 4B Rosedale Office Park
331 Rosedale Road, Albany, North Shore NZ 0632
Phone: 0800 449 725

For learning solutions, visit **cengage.com.au**

Printed in Australia by Ligare Pty Ltd
8 9 10 11 12 13 14 21 20 19 18 17

POSTERA CRESCAM LAUDE
THE UNIVERSITY OF
MELBOURNE

Evaluated in independent research by staff from the Department of Language, Literacy and Arts Education at the University of Melbourne.

Moon Bubble

George Ivanoff
Sue Dani

Contents

Chapter 1

Landings

In 1969, Neil Armstrong became the first man to walk on the Moon. Last weekend, I became the first kid to walk on the Moon. The problem is ... no one believes me.

I rang the newspaper but the reporter hung up on me.

I told my teacher but she told me to stop being silly.

I told Mum and Dad, but they just smiled and said I had an over-active imagination.

I told my best friend, but he just laughed and said: "Yeah! Right! Good one!"

Jasper is the only one who believes me. He listened to my whole story. But, he's a cat so I don't think that really counts.

So, I've decided to write down my story – the story of how I got to the Moon and back!

Chapter 2

Camping

It all started with a camping trip. Dad thought it would be fun to bring along a metal detector. He didn't really use it very much. But I did.

The metal detector beeped while I was down by the river, so I started digging. I hoped that it was gold or buried treasure – how cool!

But, it wasn't. It was a lump of shiny, silver metal shaped like an egg, about three times the size of a chicken's egg. I had no idea what it was. It wasn't exactly buried treasure, but it was mysterious. And I love a mystery …

Running Words 230

I ran back to the campsite and showed the metal egg to Mum and Dad.

"It looks very clean and new for something that was buried," said Mum.

I helped Dad light the campfire, and then he came to look at the metal egg. "I don't know what this metal is," he said, looking closely at it. "It feels really strange." He shrugged and passed it back to me.

The metal egg was smooth and shiny,
but it wasn't cold and it felt mysterious.
Maybe it was from an alien spaceship?
How cool would that be, I thought.
I could find the rest of the spaceship
and go on an adventure into space!

Chapter 3

Bubble Power

That night, after Mum and Dad went to sleep, I sat by the campfire and stared at the metal egg. I held it close to the fire to get a better look and suddenly it jumped right out of my hand! I couldn't believe it – the egg was floating in the air right in front of me.

The egg began to glow as it moved closer to the fire. When it reached the flames, it got so bright I had to cover my eyes. It was like the fire was recharging its battery.

Finally, the egg came out of the fire and floated beside me. There was a buzzing sound from inside it ... SNAP! A tiny metal arm popped out the top of the egg. On the end of the arm was a metal loop. Electricity crackled inside the loop, like lightning.

Then, something began to grow out of the metal loop – a shimmering bubble that crackled with electricity. The bubble got bigger and bigger – almost as big as my tent!

Carefully, I reached out to touch the bubble. All of a sudden, my hand went through its surface. I tried to pull it out, but I couldn't. It was like the bubble was one-way. You could get in, but not out.

Suddenly, the bubble started to move, pulling me along. I tried to run, but I tripped and ended up falling into the bubble.

A few seconds later, the egg, the bubble and I zoomed off into the night sky!

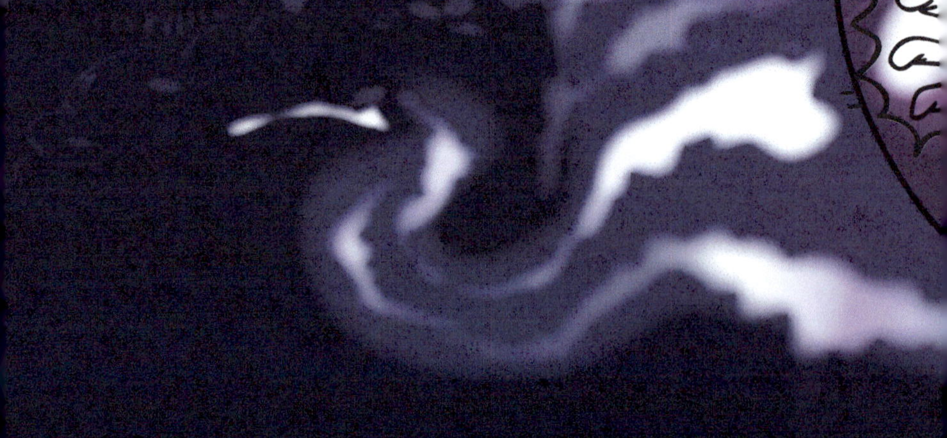

Chapter 4

To the Moon

Up and up the bubble zoomed with me inside. I was off on the adventure of a lifetime!

I could see the ground getting further away. Up and up I went, until I could see the Earth below me.

I looked ahead and I saw where the bubble was heading – to the Moon! The Moon got closer. I started to see things on its surface – mountains and huge craters.

Then, the bubble started to slow down as it flew over the Moon's surface. In the distance, I could see a shape and some colours – red, white and blue. It was a flag, the flag that Neil Armstrong planted when he walked on the Moon in 1969!

There was something on the ground beside the flag, something smooth and shiny. It was another metal egg, like the first one I found. The bubble landed right on top of it.

This egg came through the bubble's surface and I picked it up. Then, I had an idea. I pushed on the wall of the bubble. As it rolled forward I took a step, then another step and another one.

Wow! I was walking on the Moon! Cool, huh?

But five steps were all I got, because the bubble started to rise. But then, the first egg flickered, like it was running out of power, and stopped glowing. The bubble dropped back to the Moon's surface.

Now, I had wanted an adventure, but I didn't want to be stranded on the Moon! I suddenly remembered that I still had the matches from when I helped Dad light the campfire. I lit a match and held it under the new egg, desperately hoping the flame would power up the egg.

The new egg glowed brightly when the flame touched it. The bubble suddenly zoomed up, and I was flying through space again, heading back to Earth.

The bubble landed by the campsite and burst, just as the Sun was rising.

Like I said, no one believed my story. But, I've still got both eggs. And we're going camping again in a few weeks. This time, I'm going to put them in the fire before Mum and Dad go to sleep!